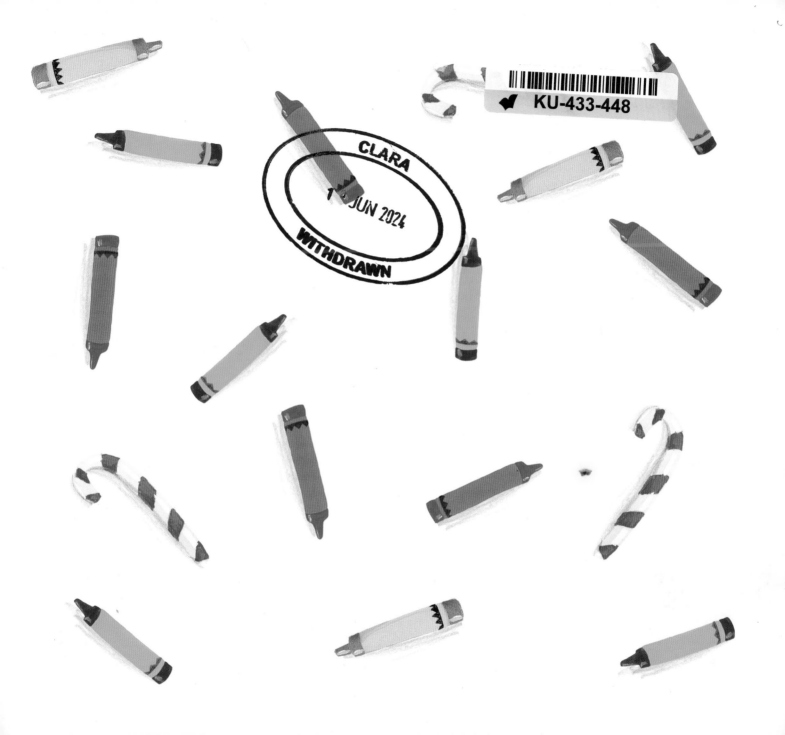

To Steven Malk and Jeff Dwyer

—D.D.

For Hannah

—O.J.

HarperCollins *Children's Books*

THE CRAYONS' CHRISTMAS

I thought WE TALKED ABOUT this!

DREW DAYWALT
OLIVER JEFFERS

One snowy December day, Duncan was making Christmas cards with his crayons when the postman brought a letter, only it *wasn't* for him . . .

From:
Mum and Dad

CRAYON
POSTAGE

6P

To: Peach CRAYon
Flat 4, CRAYon BOX
Duncan's Room
on the BOOKShelf
(Next to weird pen holder)

Duncan and his crayons spent the next day playing in the snow.

Feeling snowed
out, but suddenly
very Christmassy,
the crayons
headed inside
to warm up
and get out the
decorations.

You know I'm candy, right, Duncan? And you know you're supposed to eat candy, right? Because, last time I checked, people didn't Hang candy on the tree TEN YEARS in a ROW! I'm older than you are, kiddo.

NOW, will someone please EAT ME and end this MADNESS?

FREE at LAST!! I was in there a whole year.

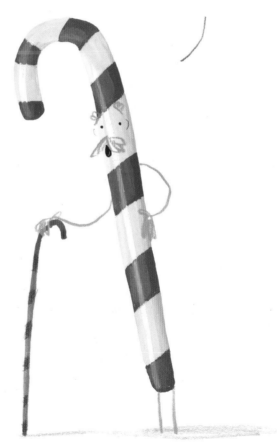

The next day, as Duncan and the crayons decorated the house, they heard a knock on the door . . .

Can I please NOT be on the Back of the Tree Facing the WALL this year?

It was the postman with another letter!
This one was addressed to Beige Crayon.

BEIGE senior

CRAYonton

Pencilvania

BEige CRAYon

The CRAYON BOX

Top of the Bookshelf

DUNCan's ROOM

And you know what? The next night, they made Beige's Dad's World-Famous Top-Secret Gluten-Free Christmas Cookies and Hot Cocoa!

Ahhh... Feel that stress just melt away.

Just as they set out the cookies and cocoa, another letter came in the mail. This one was from Grey Crayon, who was away visiting his family.

GREY CRAYON
GREYS land
TeNNeSSee

DUNCAN'S cRayons
The CRAYon Fort

WHerever Duncan
LEFt it

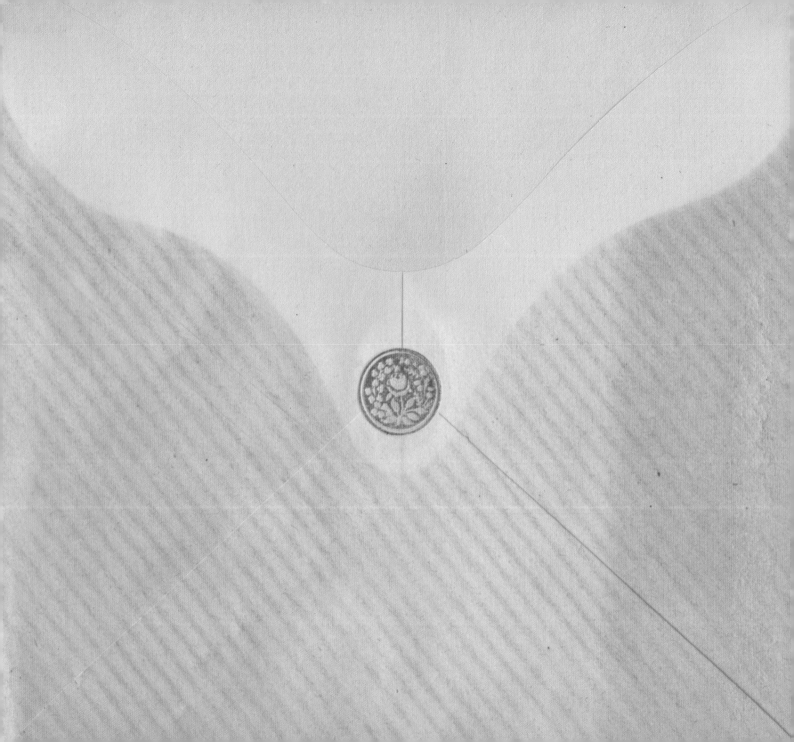

After such a great present from Grey, the crayons remembered they had some presents of their own to wrap!

With the presents all wrapped, it was time to go carol singing!

HALLS with
CRAYONS,
la la la LAAA!!

Just as the crayons came home from carol singing,
the postman delivered a big package for . . .

. . . Chunky Toddler Crayon!

OOH! I ordered this CHRIStmas GIFT on line.

Thats How it works, Right? You order gifts for yourself? It's NOT? oh... sorry! Well, the good news is that we can all play with it. open it and see...

CRAYONS
EXPRESS

Non PRIORITI
SHIPPing

SHIPPING ADDRESS

CHUNKY   TODDLer CRAYON
Flat 7, CRayon BOx
DUNCAN'S Room
on the BOOKShelf

NOTES:
next to weird pen holder

Finally, it was Christmas Eve, time for the big Christmas play!

After the play, at the end of the night, there was a package waiting for them at the front door . . . *FROM THE NORTH POLE!!!*

But it *wasn't* from Santa . . .

From:
Esteban
(The Magnificent)
& Neon Red, too!

To:
Duncan and EVERYONE
BACK HOME

VIA AIR MAIL

Duncan was happy that his crayons had received such wonderful gifts. All he had were letters from Grey, Esteban and Neon Red saying they wouldn't be home for Christmas. That made him sad and no one in the world noticed or cared . . .

Except for the crayons! In this season of giving, they decided to give back to the boy who had always given them love, respect and even a home.

YAY! Finally!

ALSO BY DREW DAYWALT AND OLIVER JEFFERS:

The Day the Crayons Quit

The Day the Crayons Came Home

First published in the USA by Penguin Workshop, an imprint of Penguin Random House LLC, in 2019
First published in hardback in Great Britain by HarperCollins *Children's Books* in 2019

13 5 7 9 10 8 6 4 2

ISBN: 978-0-00-818036-2

HarperCollins *Children's Books* is a division of HarperCollins*Publishers* Ltd.

Visit our website at: www.harpercollins.co.uk

Manufactured in China

The art for this book was made with crayons, the Postal Service and a cardboard box.